MARTHA SPEAKS™

Summer Fun

Three Stories in One

Based on the characters created by Susan Meddaugh

Houghton Mifflin Harcourt
Boston • New York • 2013

WGBH *Martha Says It with Flowers* © 2010 WGBH Educational Foundation and Susan Meddaugh
Pool Party © 2011 WGBH Educational Foundation and Susan Meddaugh
Leader of the Pack © 2010 WGBH Educational Foundation and Susan Meddaugh

For information about permission to reproduce selections from this book,
write to Permissions, Houghton Mifflin Harcourt Publishing Company,
215 Park Avenue South, New York, New York 10003.

ISBN 978-0-547-97025-7
Design by Rachel Newborn, Stephanie Cooper, and Bill Smith Group
www.hmhbooks.com
www.marthathetalkingdog.com
Manufactured in China
SCP 10 9 8 7 6 5 4 3 2 1
4500394040

In the beginning . . .

Is the world ready for Martha?

Pool Party

Adaptation by Karen Barss

Based on the TV series teleplay written by Melissa Stephenson and Raye Lankford

Based on the characters created by Susan Meddaugh

"This is a great idea, Truman!" said T.D.

Truman had coated playing cards with plastic so they could play games in the pool in his backyard.

"Yes," Helen agreed. "When it's this hot, a pool is the only place I want to be."

Alice rushed into the yard.

"Sorry I'm late," she said. "I had to get a new tube of sunscreen so I wouldn't get sunburned."

Alice slathered her arms, legs, and face with sunscreen.
Then she jumped into the pool with a big splash.

"I put on sunscreen too," Helen said. "It's a good idea."

"My skin is so fair, I burn really easily," said Alice.
"I can't take chances, especially since Tiffany's pool party is tomorrow!"

The friends climbed out of the pool and ran through the sprinkler. Alice started rubbing sunscreen on her face and arms.

"Uh . . . you just finished doing that," said T.D.

"It might have washed off," Alice said.

Then they played badminton. Alice stopped abruptly to put on more sunscreen.

"Again?" asked Helen.

"I might have sweated it off," replied Alice.

At lunchtime, Alice squeezed more lotion on her arms, legs, and face.

"Don't tell me you ate it off," said Truman.

Alice shrugged. "I'm not the sort of kid who takes chances."

The friends played duck, duck, goose, wearing sunglasses in the bright sun.

T.D. walked around the circle, "Duck . . . duck . . . duck . . ."

When he got to Alice, he stopped and gasped!

The other kids raised their sunglasses and stared.

"Alice," T.D. said slowly. "You should get out of the sun."

"What? Am I red?" asked Alice.

"Not exactly," T.D. replied. "Sort of a bronzy . . . browny . . . orange."

Alice took off her sunglasses and gasped.

"This is the worst sunburn ever!" And she grabbed her
T-shirt and ran home.

Alice's mother looked at her skin, shaking her head.

"It's not sunburn. It's dye. Like the stuff you use to color Easter eggs," she explained.

"You bought a self-tanning suncreen by mistake," her mother said. "It has a chemical that dyes your skin."

"But who would want to be dyed orange?" Alice asked.

"I think that only happens if you use too much," her mother replied.

"I have to get this off!" Alice said later that afternoon. "I can't go to Tiffany's pool party looking like an orange Easter egg!"

"I have an idea," T.D. said.

"Me too," said Truman.

And they both left.

Truman returned with a jar.

"I brought you some of my mom's body scrub. It says, 'Removes old skin and produces a fresh, dewy glow in minutes.' "

Alice grabbed the jar and scrubbed. But she was still orange.

T.D. appeared with a bowl of lemon wedges.

"My grandma says lemons fade freckles," he explained.

Alice rubbed her arms and legs. "They aren't helping, are they?"

T.D. shook his head. "No . . . but you smell zesty!"

When the friends left Alice's house, they were disappointed.

"Alice can't miss Tiffany's pool party," said Helen. "It's going to be the best party ever!"

Suddenly, Martha perked up. "I have an idea," she said.

She whispered something to Helen. "I like it," said Helen, smiling.

Martha ran to all her friends' houses and then returned home.

"I told everyone I could think of," she reported to Helen.

"Do you think they'll do it?" Helen asked.

"Of course they will," Martha replied. "Who could refuse a talking dog?"

The next morning, Alice sat on her bed—hot, discouraged, and orange.

"Helen called to say she found a way for you to blend in," Alice's mom said.

"But Mom, I look like a gumdrop with glasses!" Alice replied.

"Just go. You'll have fun."

Alice grabbed a towel and left to change into her bathing suit, feet dragging.

At Tiffany's house, Alice reluctantly opened the gate.
She couldn't believe her eyes!

"Well? What do you think?" asked Martha, wagging her orange tail.

"We didn't want you to feel self-conscious about being orange," Helen explained.

Alice threw her arms around her friends.
"I have the best friends ever!" she said.

And they all jumped into the pool with a splash!

MARTHA SPEAKS™

Leader of the Pack

Adaptation by Emily Flaschner Meyer
Based on the TV series teleplay written by Ken Scarborough
Based on the characters created by Susan Meddaugh

"I think dogs should get an allowance," Martha said one day as she walked into Helen's room. "But Dad says no. I do chores. I clean up all the food that falls on the floor. What do *you* think?"

Helen wasn't paying attention. She was busy doing homework.

"It's a family tree," Helen said. "It shows all your relatives and how they're related."

"Ooh, ooh!" Martha cried. "Where am I? Where's Skits?"

"A family tree is made up of just people, Martha," Helen explained.

Martha was upset.

"First no allowance," she said to Skits, "and now we're not even included as part of Helen's family tree! Where's *our* family tree?"

Then Martha thought of someone who might know.

Martha and Skits went to see Kazuo, their friend from the animal shelter.

"You have a very interesting family tree," he told Martha and Skits. "I can show you your ancestors at the natural history museum."

At the museum Kazuo showed them a video about wolf packs, groups of wolves that live and hunt together.

"You are both descendants of wolves," he told them.

Martha was very excited.

"We don't need to be part of Helen's family tree!" she told Skits. "We can live like our ancestors, the wolves. It's time to find our own pack!"

Just then two neighborhood dogs ran by.

Martha gathered together Skits, the small pug Burt, and the black poodle Cisco.

"Forget your lives as pets," she told them. "From now on, we're a pack—a family—just like our wolf relatives. What is the first thing we do as a pack?"

We prowl for food!

The three dogs raced away.

Martha found them at home in front of the refrigerator.

"No, no, no!" she exclaimed. "We're not pets anymore. We're a pack. There's only one place for us now—out in the wild!"

Martha led her pack into the woods.

"This is where we prowl for food," Martha whispered. "Our ancestors worked together to hunt for their dinner."

Martha chased two squirrels up a tree. She tried to explain things to them.

"We're the hunters . . . and you're the prey," she said. "Our job is to eat you."

The squirrels' response was not surprising.

"Well," Martha said later that night, "one acorn isn't bad for our first hunt as a pack!"

But Cisco had a better idea for dinner. Across town a can was being opened. He ran home, leaving the pack behind.

"We're still a pack," Martha declared. "Look!
Here's a perfect log for our wolf den."

Burt looked at the damp hollow log. He thought
about his cozy bed at home. Then he too ran off.

"Looks like it's just you and me, Skits,"
Martha said. "We're still a pack, right?"
But it was Wednesday, and Skits's
favorite television show was on.

"I can be my own pack," Martha muttered.
Suddenly she heard something moving in a
nearby clearing. Her wolflike instincts kicked in.

Martha crept closer to the clearing.

Dinner! she thought.

She was very hungry.

But then Martha noticed that the duck had what looked like a broken wing.

Uh-oh, she thought.

Martha's stomach grumbled, and she knew what she had to do.

Martha brought the duck to the vet.

"You were right about his broken wing, Martha," said the vet. "I'll put a bandage on it."

"Will he be okay?" Martha asked.

"He'll be fine in a few weeks. Thanks for bringing him in."

Martha brought the duck home with her. She knew her family would let him stay until his wing healed. And of course they did.

"Martha," Helen said, "I want to show you something. I decided to add you and Skits to my family tree, because being part of a family is more than just being related. It's kind of like . . ."

"Being a pack?" Martha suggested.

"Thanks, Helen," she said. "And since I'm part of the family again, could I please have dinner?"

"How about some alphabet soup?" said Helen.

Martha Says It with Flowers

Based on a teleplay written by Peter K. Hirsch
Based on characters created by Susan Meddaugh

Martha was always a thoughtful dog. She was eager to please with a kind word or a helpful suggestion.

Mom said that fruitcake you made wasn't fit for a dog, but I thought it was delicious!

I'd like to add to our order. After all, what's a plain cheese pizza without bacon, pepperoni, and hamburger?

But as much as she wanted to help, some people were so hard to please, like Helen's grandmother Lucille.

Did you know these flowers aren't real?

One day, as Grandma Lucille was leaving Martha's house, she suddenly remembered something.

"Oh dear, I left my hat inside," she said.

"I'll get it!" said Martha.

She quickly returned with the hat in her mouth. But now it was crumpled and covered with bite marks and drool.

"You've ruined my hat!" cried Grandma Lucille.

I only wanted to be helpful, thought Martha. *I guess I'll have to try harder.*

"If you want Grandma to forgive you for ruining her hat, maybe you could do something nice for her on her birthday," suggested Helen.

Great idea!

The next day Martha walked into Helen's room with a muddy piece of paper in her mouth.

"I told the next-door neighbor what to write," Martha said.

Helen took the card and opened it.

"Happy one hundredth birthday," she read.

"It was kind of you to make a card, but Grandma Lucille isn't turning one hundred," Helen told Martha.

"I always have trouble figuring out age in human years," said Martha.

"Maybe you should *get* her something instead. The Wagging Tail Gift Shop might give you an idea," Helen suggested.

"Helen was right," said Martha.

She found the perfect present in an alley right next to the Wagging Tail Gift Shop.

"Grandma Lucille is going to love this!"

She saw Grandpa Bernie inside the store, and went in to show him her present.

"Martha! This is a half-eaten rotten apple!" Grandpa Bernie exclaimed.

"Really?" said Martha. "Did you notice the worm? I'd love to get this as a gift."

But Grandpa Bernie said, "You might want to get her something that a person would like."

Pleasing Grandma Lucille is not easy, thought Martha.

Martha left the Wagging Tail Gift Shop feeling very discouraged. But when she passed the butcher shop, she had an inspiration.

Dogs like it and people like it, she thought.

Skits liked it too.

"Woof!" he said.

"No," Martha told him. "This is not for us. This is for Grandma Lucille."

Bacon, the perfect present!

But when Martha brought home the bacon, Mariela said, "Oh, dear. Grandma Lucille doesn't eat bacon. We'll just save this for our breakfast tomorrow."

Skits licked his chops, but Martha was too worried to even drool. Now she had to find another present, and Grandma Lucille's birthday was coming soon.

Uh-oh. Wrong again.

I can't seem to do anything right for Grandma Lucille, thought Martha. *My gifts were all mistakes. I insulted her fruitcake. I ruined her favorite hat with the fake flowers.*

Then Martha had another inspired idea.

"Flowers," she said. "That's the perfect present!"

She got a basket and trotted off to the park with Skits.

"I know Grandma Lucille likes flowers," Martha told Skits. "She had some on her hat."

She gathered a bunch to take home.

Real flowers are always better than fake flowers!

Martha hid the flowers behind the chair in the living room for safekeeping.

The days passed quickly. Soon it was time for Grandma Lucille's birthday party!

Martha walked behind the chair to get the flowers, but . . .

Oh, no—what happened to Grandma Lucille's flowers?

They were all dry and crumbly.

"Are you ready to go to the birthday party, Martha?" Helen asked.
"Not quite," said Martha. "You go ahead and I'll meet you there."

I hope!

Martha had to get some new flowers, and fast!

It didn't take long to find a nice patch of flowers. With her basket full, Martha climbed aboard a bus that would take her close to Grandma Lucille's house.

"Those are lovely flowers," the man sitting next to Martha said.

"Thank you! They're for Grandma Lucille's birthday," said Martha. "Would you like to have one, sir?"

"How kind of you!" he said. "I'll just take this little blue one, and maybe a yellow . . ."

Good dog, Martha.

A little girl wanted a flower too, and Martha gave her one. It made the girl happy. Then Martha gave some more flowers to the other people on the bus.

"Everyone loved getting flowers. I am such a thoughtful dog," Martha said as she climbed off the bus.

So long, everyone! Have a great day!

Martha looked into her basket.

Oh, no! *Only a few flowers left*, she thought. *But they're still pretty.*

She started walking to Grandma Lucille's.

She hadn't gone far when she saw something so wonderful, she dropped her basket of flowers. It was a man dressed like a hamburger, and he was giving out free samples.

I'll just eat this hamburger and then be on my way, Martha thought.

But it was so hard to stop after only one.

"Time to go," said Martha, and she looked for her basket.

Oh, no!

Birds were carrying away the flowers.

"Stop!" yelled Martha. "It's not nice to take my flowers."

Martha looked into the basket. There was only one flower left. Then it started to rain.

When Martha got to Grandma Lucille's, she was wet and tired, but she still had one beautiful flower. Then just as the door was opened, the wind blew the petals away from her last flower.

"Happy birthday, Grandma Lucille," said Martha. "I had a whole basket of fresh flowers for you and now they're all gone, and I know how much you like flowers because of your hat, and, oh, I tried so hard . . ."

Martha was surprised when Grandma Lucille said, "Well, I'm very glad that you got rid of them. I'm allergic to *real* flowers. They make me sneeze."

A soggy Martha came inside.

"You're just trying to make me feel better," Martha said.

"No," Grandma Lucille told her. "I really mean it. But here's something I know will make you feel better."

She brought a plate from the table, and Martha discovered that she still had room for cake.

After eating her cake, Martha jumped up on the couch to take a nap.
"Oh, no," said Grandpa Bernie. "She's still wet."
But Grandma Lucille said, "That's all right. Not every family has such a considerate dog."